This is Thumper.

His parents named him Thumper because
he thumps his foot when he's thinking.

He thumps his foot when he's surprised.

He even thumps his foot when he
wants to wake someone up!

How many things can you find in the picture that start with the letter S?

DreamTivity

Wake up, sleepyheads!

It's time to start the day!

It's time for breakfast!

Mmm! The bunnies love clover.

After breakfast, it's time to play.

The bunnies begin a game of hide-and-seek.

Can you help Thumper find his sisters?
Circle them.

© Disney

It's always fun to go turtle hopping at the pond.

The turtles don't seem to mind—very much, that is!

What did the turtle say to Thumper?
To find out, begin at START and write the letters on the
lines below in the order that they appear.

,

___ ___ ___ ___ ___ ___

___ ___ ___ ___ ___ ___!

After their nap, Daisy has an idea.
"Let's visit our friends," she says.

The bunnies have lots of friends in the forest.
Here are Mrs. Opossum and her children,
who like to just hang around.

The squirrel and the chipmunk live in
Friend Owl's tree.

Here comes Mrs. Quail with her nine babies.

Mr. Mole pops up when you least expect it!

Mr. Mole has dug so many tunnels that he's lost!
Help him find his way to the pond.

© Disney

This is Flower. He is a special friend.

Friends come in all shapes and sizes!

After a day in the forest, it's time to go home.
Help the bunnies find their way.

Start

Finish

There's nothing nicer than a bedtime story
before drifting off to sleep.

Every season is different in the forest.
Can you match the name of the season with the picture?

winter   spring   summer   fall

Answers: 1-summer, 2-spring, 3-winter, 4-fall.

During the summer,
the bunnies love to sit in the sun.

Daisy loves ladybugs! How many do you see?

Answer: 8

The bunnies like to visit the pond.
The ducks swim by, all in a row.

"Time to chase butterflies!" says Trixie.

Circle the butterfly that is different.

Answer: E

Which season comes after summer? To find out, trace the lines leading from the seasons and see which one leads to Thumper.

Spring

It's fall! That's when the leaves start to change color.
Can you color the leaves on this tree red, orange, and yellow?

The forest animals start to prepare for the winter.
Squirrels collect nuts.

Some birds fly south.

Which season comes next?
Unscramble the letters below to find out.

I R W N E T

___ ___ ___ ___ ___ ___

Answer: Winter

Brrr! It's winter! That's when some of the animals hibernate. "See you in the spring!" says Flower.

Thumper and his sisters miss their hibernating friends.
But there's so much to do in winter!
Look, there's the first snowfall!

Draw lines between the snowflakes that match.

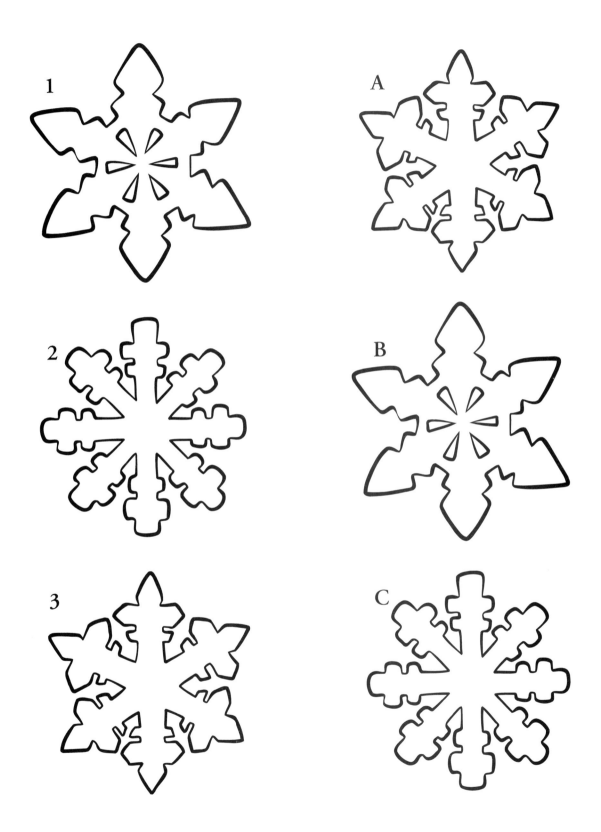

Thumper teaches his sisters how to skate on the ice.

Wheee!

One day Thumper discovers something and tells his sisters.
To find out what he says, begin at the arrow and write the letters
on the blanks in the order in which they appear.

_ _ _ _ _ _

_ _ _ _ _

Answer: Spring is here.

The sleeping animals wake up.

It rains a lot in the spring! Mushrooms make
good umbrellas—if you're a mouse, that is.

Lots of baby animals are born in the spring.
Can you match the mothers with their babies?

© Disney

There's nothing quite as cheerful
as a big, beautiful rainbow.

Hope you enjoyed your visit to the forest!
Come back soon!